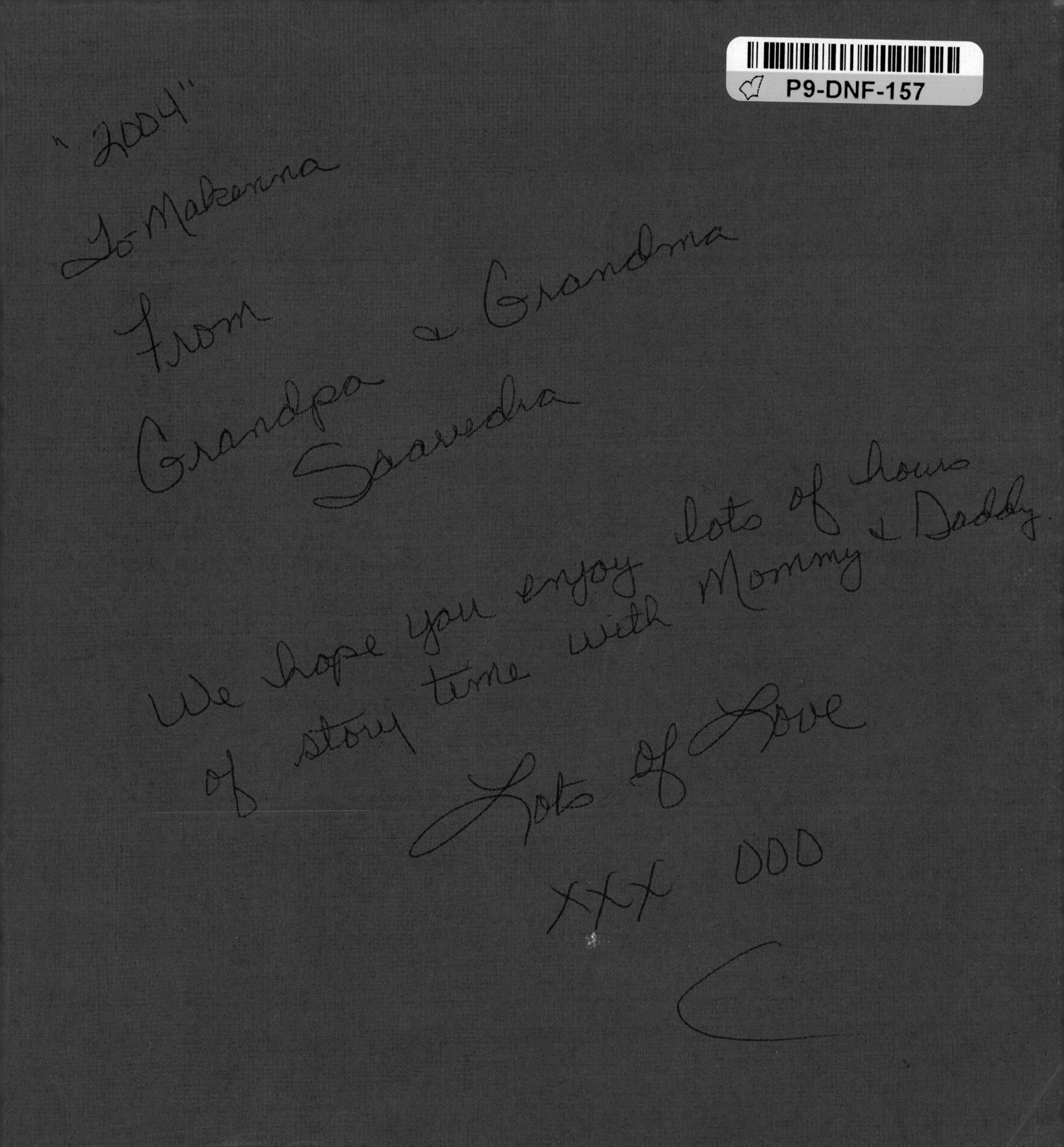
P9-DNF-157
"2004"
To-Makenna
From
Grandpa & Grandma
Saavedra
We hope you enjoy lots of hours
of story time with Mommy & Daddy.
Lots Of Love
XXX OOO

Walt Disney's Classic Storybook

New York

For more than 70 years, Disney artists have interpreted stories and characters for the printed page by creating magical storybook illustrations like the ones reproduced in this special volume.

Walt Disney's Classic Storybook contains hundreds of examples of vintage Disney storybook art from the 1950s and 1960s, recently rediscovered in warehouses. Many of these stunning pieces were never printed on quality paper, so they are presented here, close to their original color and brilliance for the very first time. They represent some of the finest examples from the Studio's golden years of book illustration, when Walt Disney enlisted his artists to draw and paint especially for children's storybooks.

Walt worked hard to ensure that this artwork lived up to his standards for quality and his desire to deliver Disney magic in a form he considered an important part of his legacy—children's storybooks.

TABLE OF CONTENTS

Designers: Deborah Boone, Alfred Giuliani
Archivist: Donna Kerley

Story based on the Walt Disney motion picture, 101 DALMATIANS, is based on the book *The One Hundred and One Dalmatians* by Dodie Smith, published by Viking Press.
Story based on the Walt Disney motion picture, DUMBO, suggested by the story, *Dumbo, the Flying Elephant*, by Helen Aberson and Harold Perl. Copyright © 1939 by Rollabook Publishers, Inc.
Story based on the Walt Disney motion picture, MARY POPPINS, is based on the series of books by P.L. Travers.

Printed in the United States of America

First Edition

7 9 10 8

This book is set in 20-point Cochin.

Library of Congress Catalog Card Number: 2001088825

ISBN 0-7868-3342-4

For more Disney Press fun, visit www.disneybooks.com

Walt Disney's

Sleeping Beauty

Long, long ago, in a faraway land, a lovely princess was born. Her hair was as golden as the sun, and her cheeks were the pale pink of the first clouds of morning.

"She is as beautiful and as full of promise as the dawn itself," said her mother and father. And after much thought, they named her AURORA, which is another way of saying Dawn.

To celebrate Aurora's birth, King Stefan invited everyone in the land to come to the castle. King Hubert and his young son, Phillip, were among the guests. During their visit, King Stefan and King Hubert planned to announce that Princess Aurora

and Prince Phillip would someday marry,

uniting the two kingdoms.

Three good fairies came to bless the baby with gifts. The first fairy, Flora, waved her wand and gave Aurora the gift of beauty. Fauna, the second fairy, gave her the gift of song. But before the third fairy could speak, the castle doors flew open.

There stood the evil fairy Maleficent. She was angry that she had not been invited to the celebration, and she placed a cruel spell upon the baby. "Before the sun sets on her sixteenth birthday, she shall prick her finger on the spindle of a spinning wheel—and *die*!"

The terrified King and Queen begged the good fairies to help. They could not undo the evil curse. Yet there was still hope. The third fairy,

Merryweather, had not yet

given the princess her gift.

Perhaps she could soften the spell.

Merryweather waved her wand

over the baby. "If through this wicked witch's trick, a spindle should your finger prick, a ray of hope there still may be in this the gift I give to thee. Not in death, but just in sleep, the fateful prophecy you'll keep, and from this slumber you shall wake when true love's kiss the spell shall break."

King Stefan ordered every spinning wheel in the land to be burned while the three fairies tried to think of other ways to keep Aurora safe. Finally, it was agreed that Flora, Fauna, and Merryweather would take Aurora away from the castle to keep her safe from Maleficent until the day of her sixteenth birthday.

And so the King and Queen watched sadly as the good fairies carried their beloved child away to a small cottage in the woods, where they would raise her as their own. The fairies changed Aurora's name to Briar Rose and vowed not to use their magic.

Years passed, and Briar Rose grew to be beautiful and good. Her lovely voice echoed through the forest when she sang.

One day, handsome Prince Phillip came riding through the woods. Suddenly he heard a young woman singing. He followed the delightful sound, and soon he met a beautiful peasant girl. Before long, the two young people had fallen in love . . . without even learning each other's name.

That day happened to be Briar Rose's sixteenth

birthday. At the cottage, the three fairies decided to use their magic to make her birthday

extra special. Flora made Briar Rose a beautiful new dress.

"We'll make it blue," said Merryweather.

"Oh, no, dear. Pink!" cried Fauna. The fairies simply could not agree on a color.

What a day it was! When Briar Rose returned to

the cottage, the fairies told her the truth about her royal birth and about her betrothal to Prince Phillip. They were stunned when the young princess burst into tears upon hearing the news. How could she marry a prince when she was in love with the young man she had met in the woods?

Meanwhile, King Stefan and King

Hubert were happily making plans for the wedding of Prince Phillip and Princess Aurora. Soon the princess would return to the castle

and the two kingdoms could be united at last. But Prince

Phillip shook his head and told his father he was going to marry a beautiful peasant girl. And off he rode to find his love.

That night, the three fairies secretly brought Princess Aurora back to the castle. But Maleficent was prepared for Aurora's return. Inside the castle, Aurora soon fell under Maleficent's evil spell. The princess followed a strange green light up a narrow stairway to a dark tower.

The three good fairies tried to stop her, but they were too late. At Maleficent's command, Aurora had pricked her finger on a glowing spinning wheel.

"You poor, simple fools, thinking you could defeat me!" Maleficent shrieked at the good fairies. "Well, here's your precious princess!" Aurora lay motionless.

Thinking quickly, Flora, Fauna, and

Merryweather cast a spell and put everyone in the castle to sleep until they could find Aurora's true love. As King Hubert drifted off to sleep, he mumbled that Prince Phillip had fallen in love with a peasant girl in the woods.

It had to be Aurora! Prince Phillip *was* her true love! The fairies set off to find the prince.

But Maleficent found him first. She dragged him to her castle and left him in chains in the dungeon.

When the good fairies finally found the prince, they set him free. "Arm thyself with this enchanted Shield of Virtue and this mighty Sword of Truth," said

Flora. Then the fairies led him out of the castle.

Maleficent tried in vain to stop the prince from getting to King Stefan's castle. She cast a spell, and thick

blackthorn bushes suddenly sprouted up, blocking Prince Phillip's way. Slashing the brambles with his sword, the prince slowly cleared a path and continued on.

Then Maleficent turned herself into a fire-breathing dragon.

"Now you shall deal with *me*!" she shouted at the prince.

The courageous prince fought the terrible beast with all his might. At last, he was able to kill it with the Sword of Truth.

Racing through the castle, Prince Phillip came to the tiny chamber where Aurora slept. Kneeling beside her, he kissed the beautiful princess.

Aurora's eyes slowly fluttered open. Recognizing the prince as the young

man she had met in the woods, a smile came to her lips.

The spell was broken. Throughout the castle, everyone began to wake up. The trumpeters were finally able to announce the long-awaited return of the princess. King Stefan and King Hubert were finally able to plan the royal wedding.

That evening there was a royal ball at the castle. Princess Aurora and Prince Phillip came down the great stairway and entered the ballroom. A cheer went up throughout the castle as they began to dance.

The good fairies looked on, overjoyed. "Oh, I just love happy endings," said Fauna. And indeed it was a very happy ending for Princess Aurora and Prince Phillip.

WALT DISNEY'S
Pedro

Once upon a time in a little airport near Santiago, Chile, there lived three little airplanes. There was a papa plane, a mama plane, and a baby plane

named Pedro. When he grew up, Pedro wanted to be a mail plane, just like his father.

So Pedro went to

ground school every day and studied hard to learn the ABCs of flying. In geography class, he learned about the mail route between Santiago and Mendoza, over the mighty Andes, past Aconcagua, the highest mountain in the Western Hemisphere. Pedro dreamed of the day when he might fly that route.

Then one morning the papa plane had a cold in his cylinder head, so he couldn't deliver the mail. The mama plane had high oil pressure, so she couldn't do it either. But the mail had to go through. There was only Pedro to take it.

"Flight Two leaving for Mendoza," chanted the signal tower.

"That's me!" said Pedro, and he swung into position on the runway.

Pedro waved a wing in the direction of his parents' hangar. Then he took off!

"Don't lose your flying speed!" he heard the signal tower call from the ground. And up into the air flew Pedro.

He had a hard time of it, struggling for altitude, but he put everything he had into it. Soon Pedro was flying over the mountains. Looking right and left, he kept a careful distance between himself and the mountain peaks.

But suddenly—oh-h-h-h-h-h! Down fell Pedro, and at such terrific speed that his muffler and cap were ripped loose.

Pedro was caught in a downdraft! He fought against the downward pull with all his strength. At last he managed to push his nose up and pull out!

Then Pedro headed into the range of snowy peaks. He was doing all right! In fact, Pedro felt on top of the world when suddenly he shuddered in every cylinder. He was face-to-face with that towering monarch, Aconcagua! And most frightening of all, the crags of the mountainside seemed

to form an evil stone face.

Taking a deep breath, Pedro shot forward, raced behind a huge cloud, and came out on the other side of the peak, safe and sound and pleased with himself. The worst was over. Now it was clear sailing to Mendoza.

Pedro came into the Mendoza airport just as he had been taught. He spied the mailbag on the hangar hook, waiting for pickup. Almost bursting with pride, Pedro rolled over on his back and floated down toward the dangling sack. He hooked it neatly over one wing, and in another moment he was flying off again.

Now Pedro was homeward bound—and he was

ahead of schedule!

Just for practice he did a few barrel rolls and loop-the-loops. He dove through clouds. He had a wonderful time. But he forgot all about being a mail plane with a job to do. He spied a giant condor, and chased the ugly bird all over the sky. Before long,

Pedro lost track of the condor in a dense fog. Before him loomed Aconcagua, shrouded in low clouds.

The oil froze in little Pedro's cylinders; his motor knocked with fright. Bravely he headed toward the peak.

Now a storm broke loose with a roar of fury. The lightning lashed out at him, rain blinded him, and the wind kept shoving him toward the mountain. Suddenly his windshield wipers shuddered, and he spun around

in midair. Before he could right himself, the mailbag dropped from his wing!

The brave little plane dove through the storm after the lost mailbag. Down he shot, into the heart of the storm, and grabbed the bag on a wing.

"Now I've got to climb!" he told himself.

Up, up into the storm Pedro climbed. More altitude! he thought. I need twenty-five thousand feet! Up and still up he fought his way. At last the altimeter hand pointed to twenty-five thousand!

Pedro leveled off and headed for home. But just as he got his nose pointed safely toward the home airport, Pedro started coughing and sputtering, and he couldn't stop it. Oh, no! He was out of gas! Poor Pedro began to fall toward the mountains.

Back at the home airport, Pedro's parents searched the empty skies in vain. They saw the blackness gather over the mountain peaks, and knew that it meant a storm. The hours passed, but there was no sign of Pedro.

Suddenly a distant whir caught their ears. They looked up hopefully. The eyes of the tower opened, and searchlights flashed into the sky.

It couldn't be—but, yes, it was Pedro!

He hit the runway headfirst, and bounced along upside down. His gas gauge was on empty, but Pedro had managed

to glide

home.

"It may not

have been

exactly a

three-point

landing," said

the proud

papa plane,

"but Pedro brought the mail through."

The papa plane unhooked the mailbag and opened

it. There was one card inside. *"Estoy divertiéndome,"* it read. "Having a wonderful time."

"Hmmm," said the papa plane. "Well, it *might* have been important."

Pedro wagged his tail and smiled proudly. And the papa plane, the mama plane, and little Pedro flew happily ever after.

WALT DISNEY'S
Once Upon
a Wintertime

It was once upon a wintertime, a long time ago. Sleigh bells were tinkling and runners were twinkling over the sparkling snow.

It seemed a perfect day to take a ride in the sleigh.

So Joe put a fur robe in the cutter, and he hitched up his spanking bays.

And Jenny put on

her warm little jacket, and her mittens, each one with a flower upon it, and a scarf for her chin, and a bonnet and all—and her stout little boots.

Then away they sped, down the country roads, between towering banks of snow.

What a fine, crisp, sparkling day it was! On the boughs above them the snowbirds sang.

The cutter's sleigh bells gaily rang, and the sound of them brought the bunnies to the doorway of their oak-tree home.

What fun! thought the bunnies. Let us go for a sleigh ride, too.

So out they jumped, and they rode away, seated on the runners of the speeding sleigh.

Soon the road curved down close beside the pond,

stretching smooth as glass to the woods beyond.

Joe drove up with the horses so smart and nice. And they sat and looked at the sparkling ice. Jenny and Joe agreed that it was just the sort of ice that was perfect for skating on. So out they hopped,

and in a trice,
their skates
were fastened;
they were on
the ice.

Joe was a
star, and he
loved to show
Jenny the way
that real skaters
go, swooping

and sliding, and gracefully gliding over the ice.

On his swift twinkling skates he did fine figure eights—or nines! Or valentines!

Jenny clapped her hands at the wonderful show. But, oh woe! Down she goes!

Now Joe could not help it; he started to smile. And it grew to a chuckle after a while.

That made Jenny furious. She got to her feet, and her face was as red as a freshly scrubbed beet.

She spun on her heel, and she skated ahead so fast that she never saw a sign that said: DANGER: THIN ICE.

Crunch! Crack! went the ice, and before Joe's eyes it broke into pieces, and Jenny's cries came back to him on the wintry air.

Joe couldn't reach Jenny, standing there, because her ice chunk was floating down, faster and faster, toward the town. And there were falls in the river ahead—steep, rocky rapids!

The birds and the bunnies were all worried, too. They fluttered and chattered and wondered what to do.

The horses stood ready to help

if they could. And now Joe had a plan that really was good!

He jumped to the sleigh. At his whistle, the team raced off through the snowdrifts. Behind them, Joe made a loop in his reins

like a cowboy's rope at the rodeo. He coiled the lasso; he let it fly. But just as it left his hand, oh, my!

Head over heels over toes went Joe, *plunkety thud* in a bank of snow! And the rope missed Jenny!

Now what to do? Joe couldn't help her. He was through, until he could dig himself out.

But the birds came swooping down through the air, and picked up the rope end lying there.

While the bunnies tied one end to Joe, who was still heels up in the bank of snow, the birds flew to Jenny on the ice. The rope dropped around her, neat and nice.

Then horses and bunnies and snowbirds all pulled Jenny back, away from the falls, up the stream and onto the pond, smooth as glass, that still stretched away to the woods beyond.

Back came Jenny, and there was Joe. And they never knew how she happened to be off the ice and back under the tree. The birds and the bunnies never told. The horses just stamped their feet with the cold, and rattled their bells and shook the sleigh, as if they wanted to be on their way.

So in hopped Jenny, and after her Joe, and off they rode toward the town below. The snowbirds sang sweetly, the horses neighed, and the bunnies hopped aboard again, for they were not afraid.

And away they went, across the frosted snow, once upon a wintertime, long, long ago.

WALT DISNEY'S
THREE
LITTLE PIGS

Once upon a time there were three little pigs who went out into the big world to build their homes and seek their fortunes.

The first little pig did not like to work at all. He quickly built himself a house of straw. Then off he danced down the road, to see how his brothers were getting along.

The second little pig was building himself a house, too. He did not like to work any better than his

brother, so he had decided to build a quick and easy house of sticks. It was not very strong, but at least the work was done. Then the two little pigs danced and sang and trotted off down the road to see how their brother was getting along.

The third little pig was building a house, too, but he was building his of bricks. He did not mind hard work, and he wanted a strong little house, for he knew that in the woods nearby there lived a big bad wolf who liked nothing better than to catch little pigs and eat them up!

"Ha ha ha!" laughed the first little pig, when he saw his brother hard at work.

"Ho ho ho!" laughed the second little pig.

"You can laugh," their busy brother replied, "but I'll be safe and you'll be sorry when the wolf comes to the door!"

The two little pigs laughed again, and they disappeared into the woods, singing a merry tune.

But as they danced along, out popped the big bad wolf! Each of

the pigs ran off to his house and slammed the door. The wolf chased the first pig to his straw house.

"Open the door and let me in!" cried the wolf.

"Not by the hair of my chinny-chin-chin!" said the little pig.

"Then I'll huff and I'll puff and I'll blow your house

in!" roared the wolf. And he did. He blew the little straw house all to pieces!

Away raced the little pig to his brother's twig house. No sooner was he in the door, when *knock, knock,*

knock! There was the big bad wolf! But of course, the little pigs would not let him come in.

"I'll fool those little pigs," said the big bad wolf to himself. And he hid behind a big tree.

Soon the door opened and the two little pigs

peeked out. There was no wolf in sight.

"Ha ha ha! Ho ho ho!" laughed the two little pigs. "We fooled him."

Soon there came another knock at the door. It was the big bad wolf again, but he had covered himself with a sheepskin, and was curled up in a basket.

"I'm a poor little sheep, with no place to sleep. Please open the door and let me come in," said the big bad wolf in a sweet little voice.

"Not by the hair of my chinny-chin-chin!" said the first little pig.

"You can't fool us with that sheepskin!" said the second little pig.

"Then I'll huff, and I'll puff, and I'll blow your house in!" cried the angry old wolf.

So he huffed, and he puffed, and he blew the little twig house all to pieces!

Away raced the two little pigs, straight to the third little pig's house of bricks.

"Don't worry," said the

third little pig to his two frightened brothers. "You are safe here." Soon they were all singing gaily. This made the big bad wolf perfectly furious!

"Now by the hair of my chinny-chin-chin," he roared, "I'll huff, and I'll puff, and I'll blow your house in!"

So the big bad wolf huffed, and he puffed . . . but he could not blow down that little house of bricks! How could he get in? At last he thought of the chimney!

So up he climbed, quietly. Then with a snarl, down he jumped—right into a kettle of boiling water!

With a yelp of pain he sprang straight up the chimney again, and raced away into the woods.

The three little pigs never saw him again, and spent their time in the strong little brick house, singing and dancing merrily.

WALT DISNEY'S
LADY

Lady was a beautiful spaniel with long silky ears and a ladylike bark. Jim Dear and Darling loved her and gave her everything a little dog could possibly want. She had her own dishes with LADY printed neatly in blue, in a wreath of pink flowers.

Lady had a bed of her own, but she preferred to sleep at the foot of Jim Dear's or Darling's bed, where she was welcome.

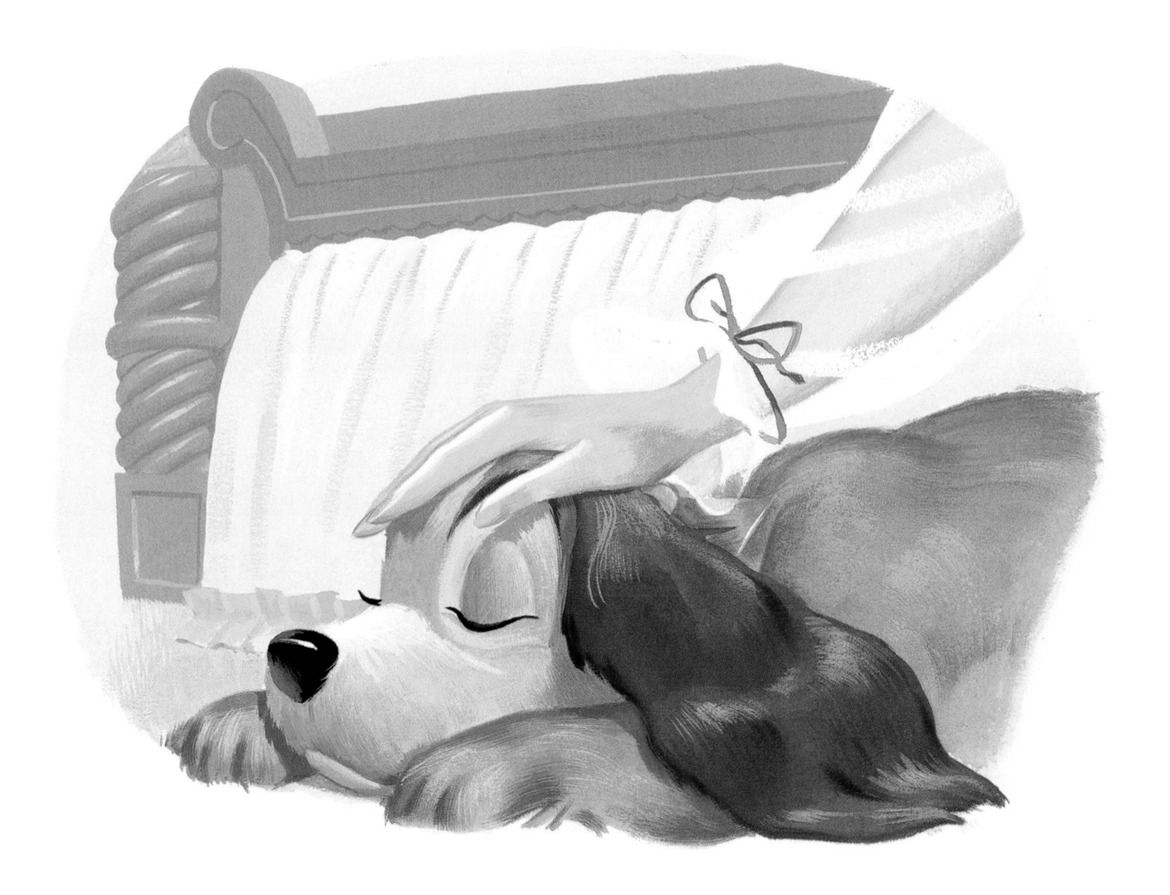

There were trips to the pet shop, where Lady's fur and nails were trimmed. She liked to look in the big mirror, and she always came away with a new bow.

When it rained, Lady wore a little red raincoat, which was the envy of the neighborhood dogs.

"Aye, she's lovely!" said Jock.

"She's the only dog I know who has a raincoat," said Trusty.

Lady had smooth bones to chew—delicious after they had been buried in the garden. But Lady never once disturbed the flower beds. That was the way she showed her family that she loved them.

"I wish I could do more for them," said Lady one day to her friends Jock and Trusty. "But what can a little dog do?"

"You could carry things for them," suggested Trusty.

"And bring things to them," said Jock.

So Lady learned to carry a package of meat. She tried hard not to tear the paper.

And she learned to catch the newspaper when the boy tossed it. When she took the paper to Jim Dear, he always patted her on the head and said, "Good Lady! Good dog!"

Lady was the happiest little dog in the whole world, until the day a baby came to live with Jim Dear and Darling. Then everything in Lady's house seemed to change. Everyone was excited and busy, and no one paid any attention to poor lonesome Lady.

"They don't love me anymore," said Lady when she told Trusty and Jock about the baby.

"Having family trouble?" It was a new voice—a rough voice. Lady looked at the strange dog.

"Families only tie you down," said the dog. "I don't

have one, and I get along fine."

The dog gave a gay whistle and off he trotted, his ears and tail waving in the breeze.

"Who is he?" asked Lady.

"His name's Tramp," said Jock.

"He's rough and a bit braggy," added Trusty. "But Tramp's really not a bad fellow."

When Lady joined her friends the next day, Tramp was with them.

"Why the tears?" he asked.

"They're so busy with the baby," sobbed Lady,

"they've forgotten my bath."

Just then Jock and Trusty were called in to dinner. No one called Lady. She felt very lonely. So when Tramp

whistled and ran after a wagon, Lady followed.

Lady never forgot that evening. What a wonderful time they had! They chased a cat up a tree. They jumped over fences. They barked at the moon.

But by and by Lady's soft little feet began to hurt. So when Tramp chased a rat down

an alley, Lady sat near a basement window and waited for him.

Lady loved to look in mirrors and shiny windows.

While she waited for Tramp to come back, she glanced at her reflection in the window. What she saw made her jump in fright. Then she hid her face in her paws.

"Oh!" she cried. "I'm

not a lady. I'm just an ugly little dog with muddy fur and a dirty, torn ribbon. I *hate* looking like this."

"You're crying," Tramp said later as he sat beside her. "What's the matter?"

"I want to go home," sobbed Lady. "Take me home, Tramp, please."

"Well," said Tramp gently, "I'll take you home if

you want me to. But I think it's a mistake."

Tramp knew a shortcut and soon they were walking up the steps of Lady's home. Jim Dear was at the door. Beyond him Lady saw dinner waiting for her—and there on a chair were her bath things.

"Lady!" cried Jim Dear. "What do you mean by running away? Don't you know we're going to need a dog to look after the baby?"

Lady gave a soft, grateful bark.

Then Tramp wagged his tail and barked *very politely*.

"Well," said Jim Dear. "Bring your friend in, Lady. I think we can use two dogs around here to help with the baby."

Lady was happy to know that Jim Dear and Darling wanted her.

And Tramp was happy to have a home with Lady. He didn't even mind bath days *too* much. But the baby was happiest of all because he had *two* dogs to play with and take care of him.

Walt Disney's
Mary
Poppins

It was morning on Cherry Tree Lane. Admiral Boom had shot off his morning cannon to give the day a proper start. Miss Lark, in the biggest house on the lane, had sent her dog Andrew out for his morning stroll.

But in the nursery at Number Seventeen Cherry Tree Lane, Jane and Michael Banks were still in bed.

"Up, up!" said Mary Poppins, their nanny, pulling back the blankets with a firm hand. "We'll have no lounging about on a super-cali-fragi-listic day."

"Super-cali-what, Mary Poppins?" asked Michael.

"Super-cali-fragi-listic, of course. If you can't think of a word that says just what you want to say, try super-cali-fragi-listic. And it *just* describes today."

That got Jane and Michael up and dressed and breakfasted in record time.

"Super-cali-fragi-listic!" sang Jane and Michael as they marched along the lane. They almost bumped into

Mary Poppins when she stopped to speak to Andrew, Miss Lark's little dog.

"Yip yap yap," said Andrew.

"Yes, of course," said Mary Poppins. "I'll go straightaway. And thank you very much."

"Yap," said Andrew.

Then taking Jane and Michael by the hand, Mary Poppins

started off the way Andrew had come.

"What did he say?" asked Jane.

"There's been a change of plans," said Mary Poppins. "Come along, please. Don't straggle." She led them at a brisk pace down narrow, twisting streets, until she stopped at the door of a small house.

Rap, rap went the parrot's-head handle of

Mary Poppins's umbrella. Mary's friend Bert opened the door.

"How is he?" Mary Poppins asked.

Bert shook his head. "I've never seen him as bad as this," he said. "And that's the truth."

Bert opened the door wide and Mary Poppins, Jane, and Michael stepped inside.

In the center of the room stood a table set for tea. Jane and Michael looked about. They could see no one there.

"Uncle Albert, you promised not to go floating around again!" said Mary Poppins. She seemed to be speaking to the ceiling. Jane and Michael looked up. There in the air sat Mary Poppins's uncle Albert, chuckling merrily.

"I—I know, my dear," said Uncle Albert, wiping a merry eye. "But the moment I start—*hee hee*—it's all *up* with me." To the children he whispered, "It's laughing that does it, you know."

Jane and Michael were trying hard to be polite. But they couldn't help it; soon they began to chuckle.

By this time Bert was rolling about, shaking with

laughter. As they watched, he rose into the air and soon was bobbing about beside Uncle Albert.

Michael's chuckle grew to a laugh. So did Jane's. Soon they were simply filled with laughter. Their feet left the floor and up they floated till *their* heads bumped the ceiling!

"I must say you're a sight, the lot of you," said Mary Poppins disapprovingly, her arms folded.

"Speaking of sight," said Bert, "it reminds me of my brother. He's got a nice cushy job in a watch factory."

"In a watch factory?" said Uncle Albert. "What does he do?"

"He stands about all day and *makes faces*."

At that, all four of them roared so with laughter that they turned somersaults in the air.

"I found a horseshoe today," said Bert, holding his sides. "You know what that means?"

"I certainly do," said Uncle Albert. "It means that some poor horse is walking around in his stocking feet."

"Now, then, Jane, Michael! It is time to go," said Mary Poppins firmly from below.

"Oh, please stay!" begged Uncle Albert. He waved at the table on the floor. "I have a splendid tea waiting for us—if you could, er, manage to get the table to . . . "

With a rattle and a bump the table began to jerk. Then up it rose through the air, cups, cakes, teapot, and all.

"Oh, splendid! Thank you, my dear," said Uncle Albert.

"Next thing, I suppose you'll be wanting me to pour," said Mary Poppins with a sigh. And up she

floated, neat as you please, without so much as a smile. The others laughed and bobbed about as Mary poured the tea.

"I'm having such a good time," said Uncle Albert. "I wish you could all stay up here with me always."

"We'll jolly well have to." Michael grinned. "There's no way to get down."

"Well, to be honest," said Uncle Albert, "there *is* a way. Just think of something sad and down you go."

But who could think of anything sad?

"Time to go home!" Mary Poppins's voice, crisp and firm, cut sharply through the laughter.

And suddenly, at that sad thought, down came Jane and Michael, Uncle Albert and Bert, *bump, bump, bump, bump* on the floor.

"Good-bye," said Michael. "We'll be back soon."

"And thank you," said Jane as they stepped outside. "We've had a lovely time."

Uncle Albert was sobbing as he waved good-bye. "It makes me so sad to see them leave."

Back home, Jane and Michael tried to tell their father about their adventure.

But Mary Poppins just said, "Children will be children," and whisked them away to the nursery.

Michael and Jane looked at each other knowingly.

"Anyway," said Jane, kicking off a slipper, "it was a super-cali-fragi-listic day."

WALT DISNEY'S

The Grasshopper and the ANTS

The grasshopper was enjoying the bright summer's day. "Oh, the world owes me a living," he sang as he danced.

Down in the hollow, the ants were hard at work.

Silly ants! thought the grasshopper as he watched. They don't know how to play!

One little ant was carrying such a big load that he could not watch his step. Down he went in the mud.

"Ha ha ha!" laughed the grasshopper. "Why don't you stop working and come and play with me?"

So the little ant left his load, and soon he was dancing and singing with the jolly grasshopper.

Down the path came the Ant Queen's procession. When she saw the ant playing with the grasshopper,

the queen's face grew stern.

"Hmm!" she said.

At the sound of her voice, the ant snatched up his heavy load and raced away.

Then the Ant

Queen turned to the grasshopper. "You'll change your tune when winter comes," she said.

But the grasshopper only laughed. And all through the summer he fiddled and he danced.

When the brown and yellow leaves whirled down, he only danced faster.

But at last all the leaves were gone, and the world was bare and cold. The grasshopper shivered in the icy wind, with nothing to eat. Then snow began to fall, and the grasshopper had no home to go to.

But the busy ants ran into their underground house and closed the door behind them. Inside, the ants prepared a holiday feast. But in the middle of the banquet, a feeble knock was heard at the door. Outside was the grasshopper, stiff with cold.

The kindly ants took him in and thawed him out.

Then up came the Ant Queen, looking stern. "Only those that work may stay," she said. "So take your

fiddle, sir, and . . . play!"

So the jolly grasshopper played and sang, "Oh, I owe the world a living!" and the ants had a lively party, while the storm raged out of doors.

Walt Disney's
Snow White
and the Seven Dwarfs

Once upon a time, a lovely Queen sat by her window sewing. As she worked, she pricked her finger with her needle. Three drops of blood fell on the snow-white linen.

"How happy I would be if I had a little girl with lips as red as blood, skin as white as snow, and hair as black as ebony," thought the Queen.

Before long, a daughter was born to the Queen,

and she was all her mother had desired. But the Queen's happiness was brief. Holding her baby in her arms, she whispered, "Little Snow White!" and then she died.

When the lonely king married again, his new Queen was beautiful, but, alas, she was jealous of the lovely princess. And as the years passed, Snow White grew even lovelier.

Every day the Queen looked into her magic mirror and asked: *"Magic mirror on the wall, who is the fairest one of all?"* If the mirror replied that the Queen was fairest in the land, all was well.

But at last came a day when the mirror replied:

"Lips blood red, her hair black as ebony, her skin white as snow . . ."

"Snow White!" cried the Queen. Pale with anger, the Queen

ordered her Huntsman to take the princess into the forest . . . and kill her! The kindly Huntsman had to obey.

Snow White had no fear of the Huntsman and went happily into the forest with him. But at last he could bear it no longer. "I can't do it!

Forgive me," he said, kneeling before her. He warned her of the Queen's plan and told her to run away.

Alone in the forest, Snow White wept with fright. Then, ever so quietly, out from the trees crept the little woodland animals. When Snow White saw them, she

smiled through her tears.

"Everything's going to be all right," Snow White said to herself. "But I do need a place to sleep at night."

Off flew the birds, leading the way. Snow White followed. At last, through the trees, she saw a tiny cottage nestled in a clearing.

"Oh, it's adorable!" she cried. "Just like a doll's house."

Snow White peeked inside. There seemed to be no one at home, but the sink was piled high with dirty dishes and everything was blanketed with dust. Snow White also noticed seven tiny chairs, and decided that seven little children must live in the cottage.

"Maybe they have no mother," said Snow White. So in she went, followed by the animals, and began to clean the cottage from top to bottom.

Upstairs Snow White found seven little beds in a row— each with a name carved on it.

"Doc, Happy, Sneezy, Dopey—

what funny names for children! Grumpy, Bashful, and Sleepy!" Snow White yawned. "I'm a little sleepy myself!"

With that, Snow White sank down across three of the little beds and fell asleep.

Meanwhile, seven little men came marching through the woods. As they came in sight of their cottage, they stopped short. Smoke was curling from the chimney, and the door was standing open!

"Something's in there!" they cried. "Who could it be?"

At last, on timid tiptoe, they all went inside to investigate.

"Why, the whole place is clean!" said Doc.

Suddenly, they heard a sound upstairs. Slowly, up the stairs they crept, seven frightened little dwarfs.

Standing in a row at the foot of their beds, they stared at the sleeping Snow White.

"Why, i-i-it's a girl!" said one of the dwarfs.

At that, Snow White woke up. "How do you do?" she said, surprised to see the little men staring at her.

Later, when Snow White insisted that they wash up for supper, the dwarfs cried out in horror. But it was worth it in the end. For such a supper they had never tasted. Nor had they ever had such an evening of fun. All the forest folk gathered around the cottage windows to watch them dance and sing.

Back at the castle, the Queen asked the mirror again: *"Magic mirror on the wall, who now is the fairest one of all?"*

And the honest mirror replied: *"In the cottage of the Seven Dwarfs dwells Snow White, fairest one of all."*

The Queen realized that the Huntsman had tricked

her. Enraged, she hurried down to a cave beneath the palace to work her Black Magic.

First she disguised herself as a toothless old peddler woman. Then she searched her book of spells for a horrid spell to work on Snow White. "Ah! A poison apple!" she decided. "With one bite of the apple, Snow White's eyes will close forever."

The next morning, Snow White said good-bye to the Seven Dwarfs as they went off to work.

"Don't let nobody or nothing in the house," warned Grumpy.

Then off they marched to the mine, where they decided not to do their regular jobs that day. Instead, they worked on a special gift for Snow White.

From the shadows of the trees, the Queen had watched the dwarfs leave. Slowly, she crept up to the cottage.

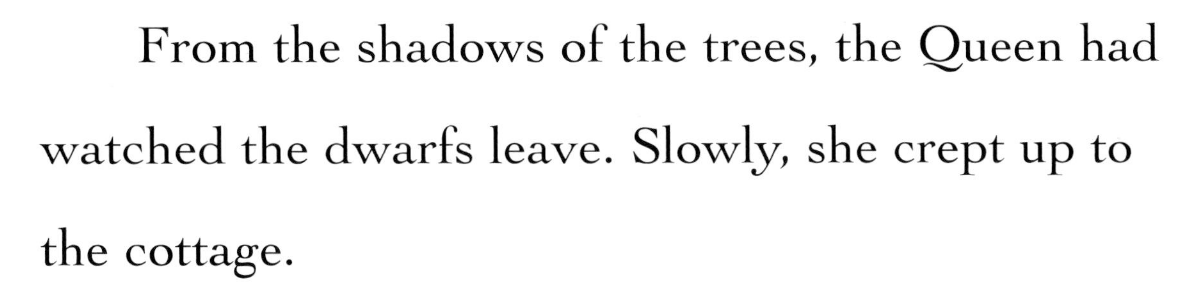

Despite the dwarfs' warning, Snow White never thought to be afraid when an old peddler woman with a basket of apples appeared outside her window. "Like to try one—hmmm?" said the wicked Queen in disguise.

The little birds tried to warn Snow White, but she

took the poisoned apple and bit into it. Immediately, she fell down onto the cottage floor.

Away went the frantic birds and animals into the woods to find the Seven Dwarfs. The dwarfs looked up in surprise as the birds and animals crowded around them. Then they realized that Snow White must be in danger. "The Queen!" they cried as they ran for home.

They were too late. They came racing into the clearing just in time to see the Queen slip away into the shadows. They chased

her through the woods until she plunged off a cliff and disappeared forever.

When the dwarfs came home, they built Snow White a bed of glass and gold, and set it up in the forest. There the Seven Dwarfs kept watch over her night and day. They were heartbroken.

After a time, the prince of a nearby kingdom heard travelers tell of the lovely maiden asleep in the forest, and he rode there to see for himself. The moment he saw her, the Prince knew that he loved Snow White

truly. He knelt beside her and kissed her lips.

At the touch of love's first kiss, Snow White awoke. The spell was broken!

There, bending over her, was the prince of her dreams.

Snow White thanked the Seven Dwarfs for all they had done to help her. Then she gave each of them a kiss and said good-bye.

Together, Snow White and the Prince rode off on a white charger to his castle, where they lived happily ever after.

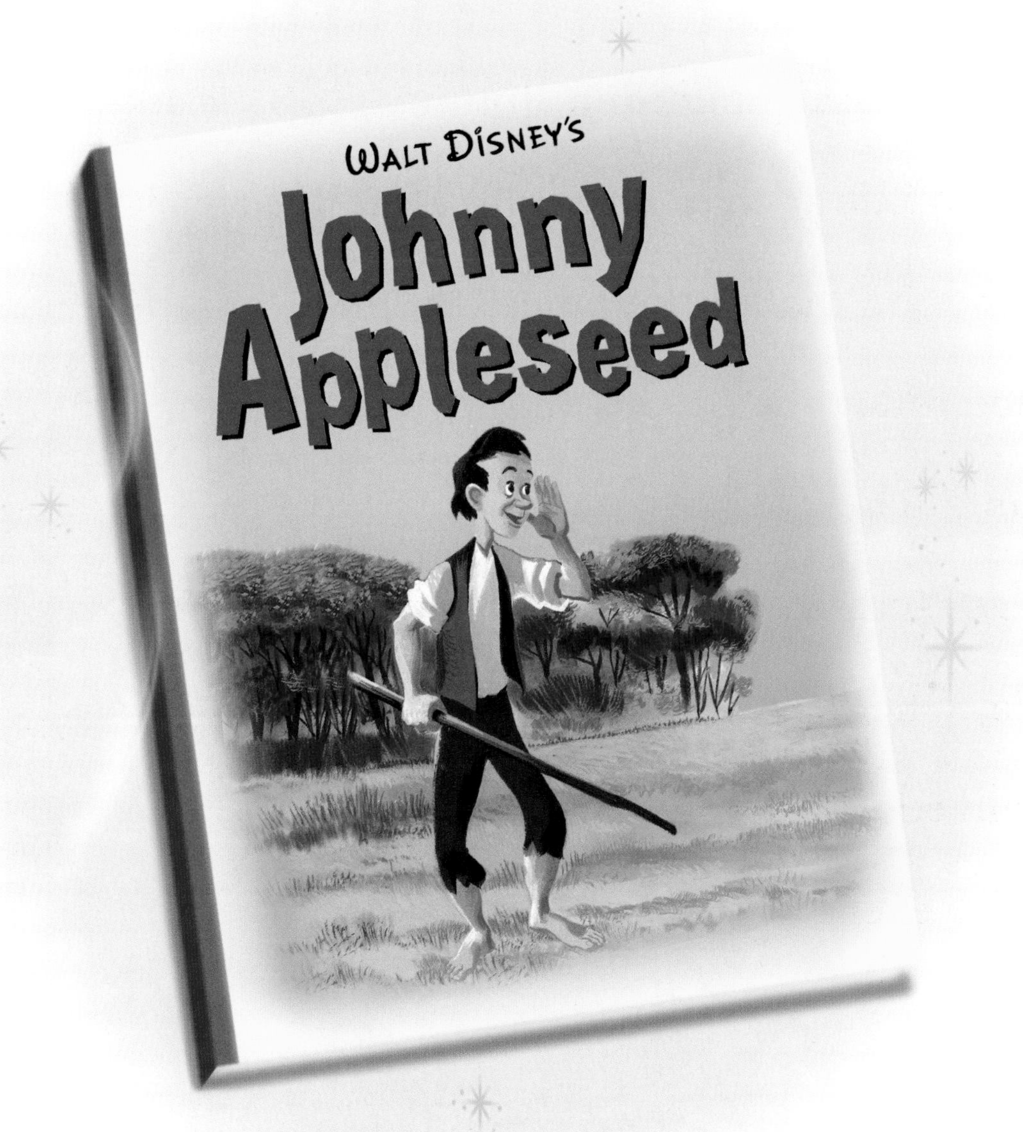
WALT DISNEY'S
Johnny
Appleseed

There was one thing Johnny Appleseed liked to do better than anything else. That was to find a sunny spot, dig a little hole, and plant an apple seed. For he knew the seed would grow into an apple tree.

"I don't know what I'll do when there's no place left for planting apple trees," said Johnny to his animal friends on the farm.

One day as Johnny was walking around his farm, looking for a spot to plant one more apple tree, along came a long line of covered wagons. Beside each wagon strode a tall, strong man with a rifle swinging at his side.

These were pioneers. With their families, they were heading off into the great empty lands of the West.

"Come West, young fellow!" they shouted to Johnny when they saw him watching from the roadside.

"But I can't be a pioneer!" said Johnny. "I'm not tall and strong. I couldn't chop down trees to build a log cabin. I couldn't clear fields to plant corn. I guess there's nothing much that I can do."

The pioneers were not listening. They were marching on. Soon they were gone.

"Oh, dear," said Johnny to himself with a sigh. "I wish I could go West, too."

"You can, Johnny!" said a voice beside him. It was his Guardian Angel! "Not all pioneers have to cut

down trees. You can be a pioneer who plants them. Why, just think of the things that apples make. There are apple pies and apple fritters, apple cores to feed the critters, and tasty apple cider. You're needed in the West, Johnny Appleseed!"

"But I have no covered wagon," said Johnny. "I have no knife and gun."

"All that you need," said the Guardian Angel, "is a little pot to cook in, and a stock of apple seeds—and the Good Book to read!"

"That's wonderful!" said Johnny. "I can start right away. I'm off for the West, Mr. Angel, this very day!"

The West was mostly forest in those days. And that forest

was big and deep and dark. But Johnny never once thought of being afraid. He marched along the forest trail, singing a merry song and watching for spots to plant his apple seeds.

No, Johnny was not afraid, but he was lonely. It had been some days since he had seen a single pioneer. And he missed his animal friends, back on the farm.

But Johnny only *thought* he was alone. On every

side, bright little forest eyes kept watch as he marched along.

For the animals did not like Men. The only Men they knew cut down trees to build cabins and shot wild animals for food and fur. Naturally, the forest folk did not like that.

So they hid and watched as Johnny Appleseed came down the path.

"He doesn't look like the others," whispered a chipmunk.

"Still, he is a Man," the gentle deer reminded them, "so we must be very careful."

At last, Johnny came to a sunny open spot among the trees, and there he stopped.

"This looks like a right nice spot for me to plant an apple tree," he said.

So Johnny set down his things and picked up a long, straight stick that was lying on the ground. "This is a fine straight stick for digging my little holes," he said.

But the animals watching thought it was a gun. "Danger!" they whispered. At the signal, the animals ran off in all directions. Oh, no!

A bunny got caught in a twisted vine. He squirmed and wriggled, but he could not free himself!

"Is someone there?" called Johnny Appleseed. For he had heard the forest folk racing away. "It would be nice to find a friend," said Johnny to himself. He called again. But there was no answer.

Pushing the bushes aside with

his long stick, Johnny Appleseed stepped into the forest. And there, while the watching animals held their breath in fright, he found the trapped bunny.

"Well," said Johnny softly. "What has happened to you, little fellow?" Gently, he untwisted the vine from around the bunny, and set him free.

"I wish you wouldn't run away," said Johnny Appleseed to the bunny. "It is lonely in the forest for me, and I would like to be friends."

The bunny did not say a word, but he put his nose into Johnny's hand and twiddled his whiskers in a friendly way. The other animals were amazed!

"Why, this Man is not bad," they said. "He is friendly."

And soon Johnny was surrounded by new forest friends. From that day on, Johnny Appleseed was never lonely again. He wandered on through the West, planting his apple seeds and singing his merry songs.

As the years passed, there were more and more

farms through the wide land. And in almost every farmyard there were apple trees. Johnny Appleseed was a welcome guest in all these farm homes.

But most of the time, Johnny kept on the move.

And as he came singing along, out from behind the bushes and trees came squirrels and deer and bunnies and all the other forest folk.

"This is the Man," they would whisper. "He carries no knife, and he carries no gun. He is a friend to us all."

Walt Disney's
The Tortoise and the Hare

It was the day of the big race. All the forest folk were there to watch. For poky old Tortoise was to race cocky, speedy Max Hare.

The Tortoise did not look like much of a racer. In fact, many of the animals thought he didn't stand a chance against Max Hare.

The contestants came out, shook hands, and crouched at the starting line.

One, two, three! and the starter's gun barked! Away streaked Max Hare! But where was the Tortoise?

He was spinning round and round on his shell! At last off he plodded down the track.

Zip! Over the hill and around the bend, the Hare flashed by like a streak of light. Meanwhile, the Tortoise was way, way back, almost out of sight.

Cocky Max Hare decided he could take time out for a nap.

When the Tortoise plodded by, Max Hare was still asleep. On plodded the Tortoise, slowly but steadily.

And on slept cocky Max Hare! As he dreamed, the Tortoise inched closer and closer to the finish line.

At last Max Hare stirred. His eyes opened wide. "How long have I been asleep?" he wondered.

What was this? From over the hill came the sound of cheers. Could it be?

The Tortoise was on the home stretch! The animals in the crowd could not believe their eyes!

But wait! Over the hill came a streak of light! It was Max Hare! Now the Tortoise really *hurried*!

The race was too close to call! The Tortoise had a huge lead. But Max Hare was gaining fast!

In the end, the race went right down to the wire—each contestant stretching and reaching for the finish line. The tape broke at the winner's touch! It was the Tortoise! Old Tortoise had won by a neck!

Now the crowd really went wild. Up on their shoulders went the Tortoise. And in the shadows, Max Hare slunk away by himself—cocky Max Hare, who had let the poky Tortoise beat him in a fair and square race.

WALT DISNEY'S
The Mad Hatter's
TEA PARTY

There was once a Mad Hatter, a peculiar fellow who lived in a strange little house in the woods of Wonderland.

Nearby lived a friend of his, the March Hare. One day the March Hare heard that it was the Mad Hatter's birthday. So he baked a birthday cake. Then down the woodland path he went, singing: "*The very merriest birthday to you! The very merriest birthday to you!"*

The Mad Hatter was delighted. He called in his friend the Dormouse, a sleepy little soul, and what a jolly time they all did have! They decided a birthday party was the best of all possible fun.

Next day, the Mad Hatter kept thinking of that party. He did wish they could have another.

The March Hare was thinking about it, too. How he longed for another piece of birthday cake! And the sleepy Dormouse wished for another cup of tea.

But it was nobody's birthday that day.

"Oh, me!" said the March Hare. "It really isn't fair.

Only one birthday a year for each of us, and three-hundred sixty-four un-birthdays!"

"Three-hundred sixty-four un-birthdays!" cried the Mad Hatter. "Well, fine! Let's celebrate those!"

So they did. Every day they had an un-birthday party. What fun!

They would set up the table and hang up the decorations and have birthday cake and tea. And after the party they would clear everything away. But that soon got tiresome.

So they set up a great long table underneath the trees. After that they never cleared anything away. Whenever things got

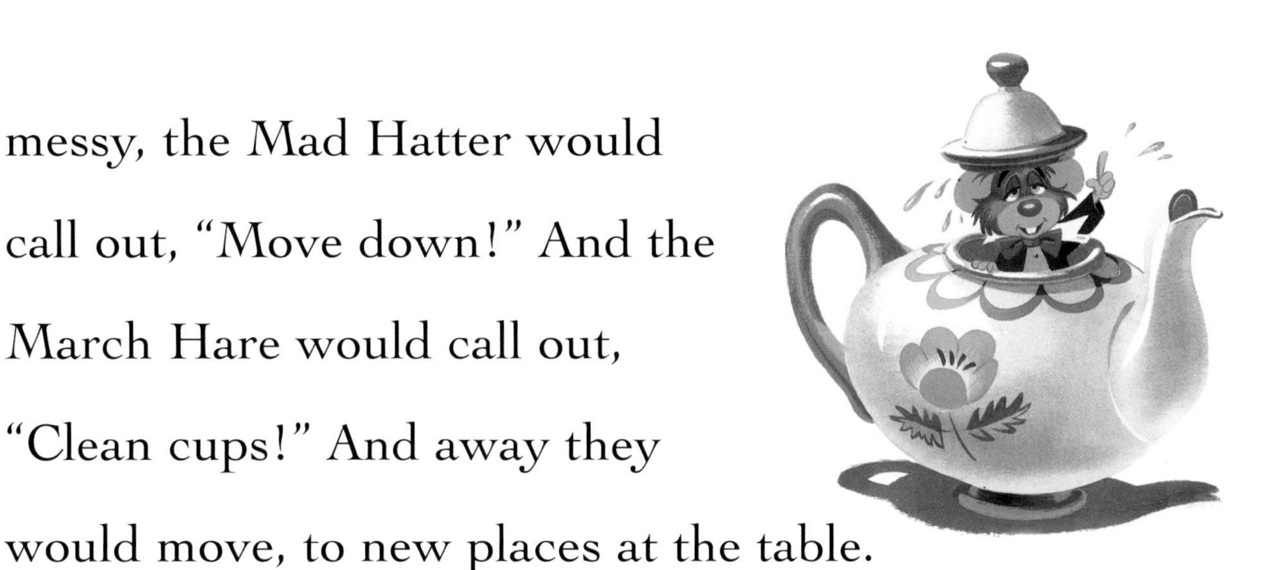

messy, the Mad Hatter would call out, "Move down!" And the March Hare would call out, "Clean cups!" And away they would move, to new places at the table.

And every day they happily sang: *"A very merry un-birthday to you! A very merry un-birthday to you!"*

All that moving got to be too much for the sleepy Dormouse. Since he was so fond of tea, he just chose himself a teapot, climbed in, and stayed. Now and then he would open a drowsy eye and join in a bit of fun.

One day a little girl named Alice wandered into Wonderland.

As she walked by herself through the Wonderland Woods, seeing most unusual sights, she began to hear singing off through the trees.

"It sounds like a birthday party," she thought. So she hurried along to see.

In through the Mad Hatter's gate she stepped. She saw the colored lanterns hanging from the trees, and the cakes upon the table. And she heard the jolly song: *"A very merry un-birthday to you! To who? A very merry un-birthday to you!"*

Then the Mad Hatter saw her.

"No room!" he cried. "What are you doing here?"

"I heard you singing through the woods," said Alice, "and it sounded so delightful—"

"It did?" cried the Mad Hatter. "What a charming child. Sit down, sit down."

"Whose birthday is it?" Alice asked.

"No one's. It's an un-birthday party," they said, and explained.

"Why, then it's my un-birthday, too," Alice said.

"A very merry un-birthday to you!" chorused the Mad Hatter and the March Hare.

"My," said Alice, "I wish Dinah were here to see this."

"And who is Dinah?" the March Hare asked.

"Dinah is my cat," Alice said.

"Cat! Cat! Cat!" cried a horrified voice. And the Dormouse, at the sound of that dreaded word, popped out of his teapot, up into the air.

"Would you like some more tea?" the Mad Hatter asked Alice.

"How can I have more," asked Alice, "when I haven't had any yet?"

"Move down!" cried the March Hare just then. "Clean cups!"

"Move down!" scolded the Hatter, rudely pushing Alice out of her chair.

"This is the silliest party I've ever seen," said Alice. "I'm going home!"

She stalked out the gate and off through the woods. No one seemed to notice that she had left.

There they are, singing, to this very day, drinking cups of un-birthday tea. If you should wander through Wonderland, perhaps you will hear voices singing loud and free—*"A very merry un-birthday to you! To who? A very merry un-birthday to me!"*

Walt Disney's
SCAMP

Lady was the mother. Tramp was the father. Their puppies were the finest ever. They were sure of that.

Three
were as gentle
and as pretty
as their
mother.

But the
fourth little
puppy—

Where is
that puppy?
Where is that Scamp?

At mealtime, three little, gentle, pretty puppies would line up, waiting for their bowl.

But the fourth little puppy, that Scamp of a puppy, would rush in ahead of them all.

At playtime, three little, gentle, pretty puppies would play with

their own puppy toys.

But the fourth little puppy, that Scamp of a puppy, would nibble at anything.

At bedtime, three gentle, pretty puppies would snuggle down to sleep.

But the fourth little puppy, that Scamp of a puppy, chose that time to learn to howl, loud and long.

One day, the four little puppies started off for a picnic with nice puppy biscuits for lunch.

Three little puppies went straight to the park and hunted for a nice, green, shady spot.

But the fourth little puppy, that Scamp of a puppy, went off on an adventure.

He found some new playmates.

Their game looked like fun.

But *Sss-ss-sst!* They didn't want Scamp to play.

So Scamp got out of there.

He found another playmate. It was a busy gopher, digging as fast as it could dig.

"Looks like fun," said Scamp. "How did you learn to do it?"

"By digging," Mr. Gopher said.

So Scamp dug, too. He dug and dug and dug.

And what do you think he found?

A big, juicy bone. It was a great big bone for a small dog. Scamp pulled at it. He tugged and hauled. Finally he got the bone out of the ground. He tugged

that bone all the way to the park.

Just as Scamp got there, a big bad dog was saying, "Ha! I smell puppy biscuits."

So he sneaked up on those three little puppies and took their puppy-biscuit lunch.

Poor little puppies! They were really very hungry. And they felt very sad.

Just then, who should appear but the fourth little puppy, that Scamp of a puppy.

He was tugging his great big bone!

"Hi, folks," he said. "Look what I found. How about joining me?"

So they ate the big, juicy bone for lunch. And they all had a fine time.

When picnic time was over, those three pretty puppies all went happily home.

And the fourth little puppy, that Scamp of a puppy, walked proudly at the head of the line.

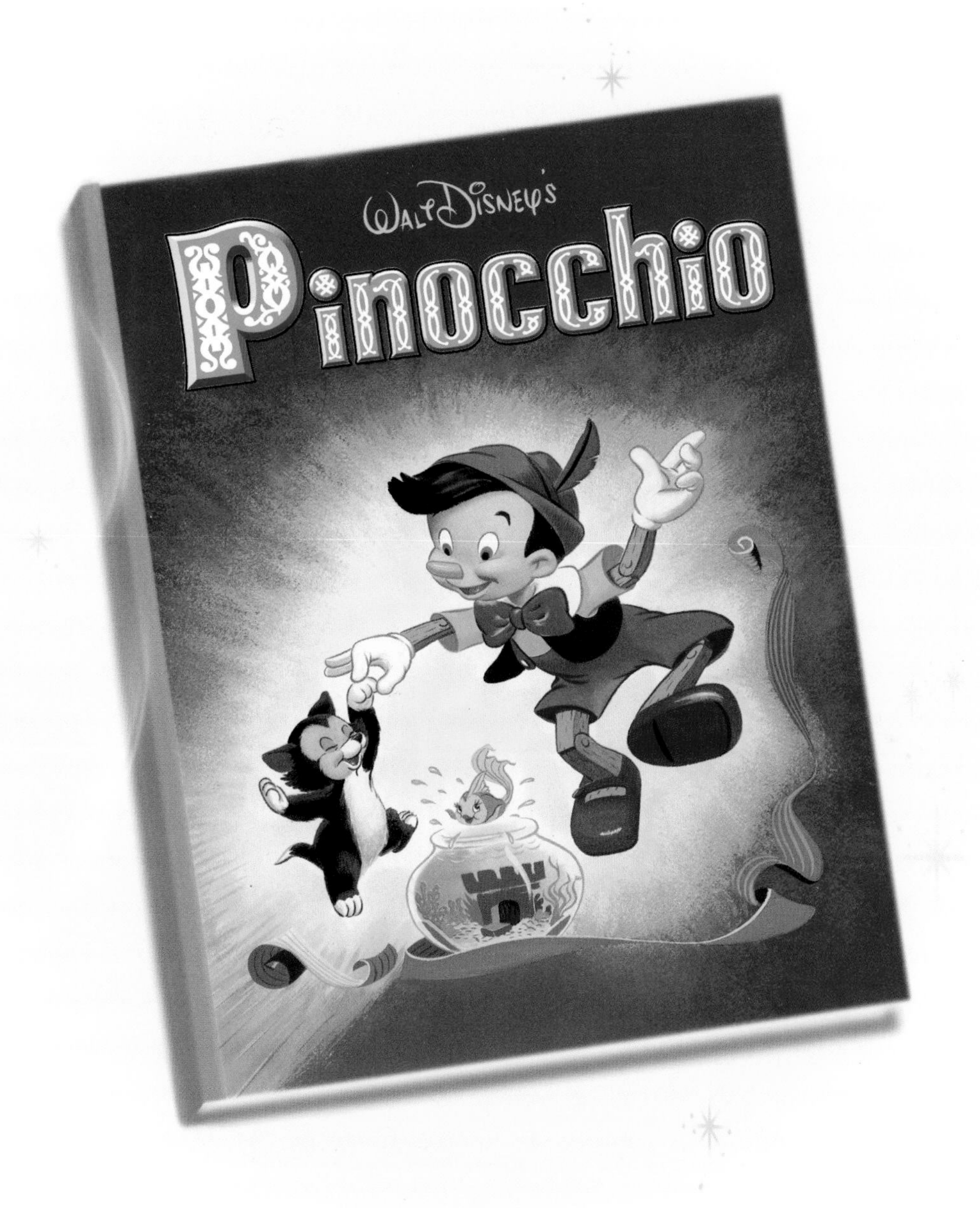
Walt Disney's
Pinocchio

One night, long ago, the Wishing Star shone down upon a tiny village, where a kindly old woodcarver named Geppetto was making a merry-faced little puppet named Pinocchio. The wooden puppet looked so lifelike!

As Geppetto climbed into bed, he made a wish: "I wish Pinocchio were a real, live boy." Then he fell fast asleep.

Hidden behind the hearth, Jiminy Cricket overheard Geppetto's wish. He felt sad because he knew the wish could never come true.

Suddenly, a bright light filled the

room and out of the light stepped a beautiful lady dressed in blue!

The Blue Fairy raised her wand and magically brought Pinocchio to life. "Prove yourself brave, truthful, and unselfish," she said to him, "and someday you will be a real boy." Then, to help Pinocchio stay out of trouble, she dubbed Jiminy Cricket the keeper of Pinocchio's conscience.

The next morning, Geppetto could not believe his eyes. His wooden puppet was laughing and running about the workshop!

Geppetto was so happy! He wanted to take good care of Pinocchio.

"You must go to school," said Geppetto, "to learn things and get smart."

So off Pinocchio went, full of good

intentions. Meanwhile, Jiminy Cricket had overslept! He caught up with Pinocchio just as the silly puppet was walking off arm-in-arm with a pair of scoundrels: Foulfellow the Fox and a cat called Gideon. They had convinced Pinocchio to become an actor rather than go to school. Jiminy Cricket tried to tell Pinocchio he was being foolish as he followed along loyally to a marionette theater.

The owner, Stromboli, marveled at Pinocchio. "A puppet without strings!" Stromboli handed Foulfellow a bag full of money. Then Foulfellow and Gideon trotted away, leaving Pinocchio behind.

That night, Pinocchio was a huge hit in the puppet show. A puppet without strings! It was a miracle!

After the show, Pinocchio said good night to

Stromboli. But Stromboli locked Pinocchio in a birdcage. “There!” he cried. “This will be your home!”

When Jiminy Cricket came backstage, he was shocked to find Pinocchio locked up.

“Oh, Jiminy,” Pinocchio sobbed. “I should have listened to you.”

Suddenly, the Blue Fairy appeared before them. "I'll forgive you this once," she said to Pinocchio. "But remember, a boy who won't be good, might just as well be made of wood."

Then she waved her wand, and Pinocchio was free!

Pinocchio and Jiminy Cricket ran for home, when who should they meet but Foulfellow and Gideon! The sly fox pretended to be shocked when Pinocchio told him how Stromboli had treated him. Before Jiminy knew what had happened, Foulfellow had persuaded the puppet to take a vacation on Pleasure Island.

Jiminy Cricket tried to remind Pinocchio of his promise to go home. But Pinocchio went ahead anyway and boarded a coach bound for Pleasure Island. It was driven by an evil-looking Coachman, pulled by a team of donkeys, and filled with noisy boys. Once again, Jiminy Cricket followed along faithfully.

The streets of Pleasure Island were paved with cookies and lined with doughnut trees. "Have a good time—while you can!" the Coachman urged the boys. And they did. Pinocchio made friends with the worst of the boys, a bully named Lampwick, and he was always in the middle of mischief.

Before long, Pinocchio and Lampwick began to sprout donkey ears! They had been lazy, so they were turning into donkeys. Jiminy Cricket gasped when he saw them.

They had to get off of Pleasure Island! But around a corner, they came face to face with the Coachman. He was herding a bunch of donkeys wearing boys' hats and shoes!

Pinocchio and Jiminy Cricket managed to get away and clamber up the wall surrounding the island. But when they looked down, they saw a little donkey in Lampwick's clothes. With a lump in his throat, Pinocchio followed Jiminy and dove into the sea.

They had a long, hard journey home, and it was winter when they came to the village. There they were surprised to find Geppetto's workshop locked and dark.

Just then, a gust of wind blew a piece of paper around the corner. It was a letter from Geppetto! He

had heard that Pinocchio had gone to Pleasure Island and had set off in a boat to find him. But a giant whale called Monstro had swallowed the boat, and Geppetto was trapped inside the whale's belly.

"I've gotta go to him!" Pinocchio declared, desperate to save his father.

A soft voice replied, "I will take you," and out of the sky fluttered a white dove. Magically, the dove grew until it was large enough to carry Pinocchio and Jiminy Cricket on its back. Then off they flew to the seashore. Pinocchio had no idea that the dove was the Blue Fairy in disguise, and that she had also brought him Geppetto's letter.

When they reached the sea, Pinocchio tied a big stone to his donkey tail. He smiled bravely at Jiminy, and together they leaped into the ocean. Down, down, down they went, through the green water to the sandy bottom.

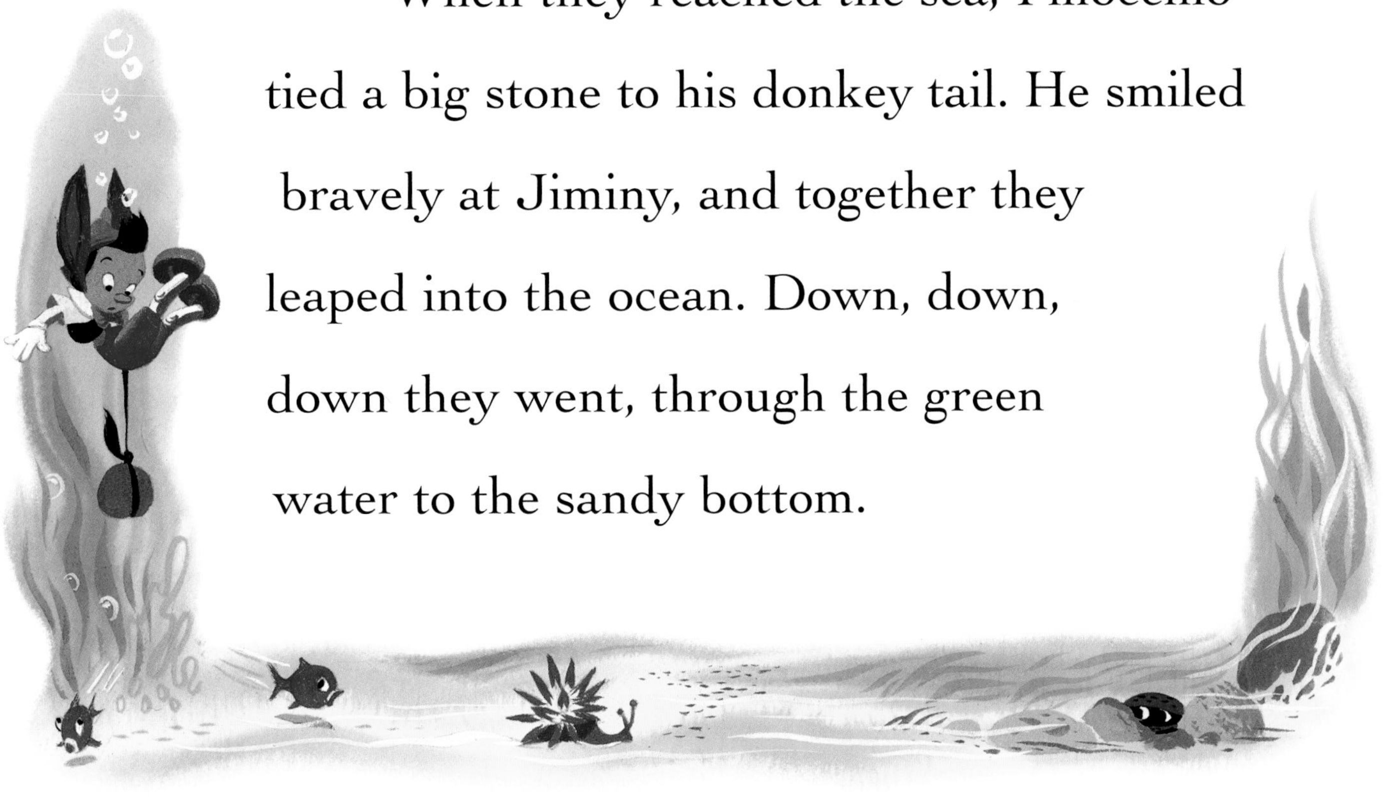

"Father!" called Pinocchio. "Father!" He and Jiminy started off, peering into every grotto and green sea cave.

Nearby was the whale they were looking for, fast asleep. Inside the whale, Geppetto was fishing. But now that Monstro was sleeping, no fish came in.

"Not a bite for days," said Geppetto to his cat, Figaro. "We can't hold out much longer."

Suddenly, Monstro gave an upward lunge, and through his jaws rushed a wall of water. With it came fish—a whole school of tuna! Nearby, Pinocchio saw the sea creatures fleeing and Monstro coming at him. Then he, too, was sucked inside the whale. Only Jiminy Cricket was left outside.

Meanwhile, Geppetto was pulling fish after fish out of the water. He was so busy, he scarcely heard a shrill cry of "Father!"

"Pinocchio? Is it really you?" said Geppetto.

Pinocchio turned away in shame when Geppetto noticed the hated donkey ears. But Geppetto said comfortingly, "Geppetto has you back again. Nothing else matters."

Pinocchio had an idea. "Quick, Father, help me build a fire!" said Pinocchio. As the fire began to smoke, they prepared a raft. Then, as the whale let out a monstrous sneeze, they sailed past the crushing jaws

and into the open sea!

But the angry whale saw them and splintered their raft. Geppetto felt himself sinking. Pinocchio swam to him and kept him afloat. Finally, they were all washed onto the beach, along with Jiminy, Figaro, and Geppetto's goldfish, Cleo. Gratitude filled Geppetto's heart. Then he saw Pinocchio lying beside him, cold and pale! The old man gathered poor Pinocchio into his arms and started home.

When he reached his home, Geppetto knelt down and prayed. Suddenly, a light pierced the gloom and a soft voice said, "Prove yourself brave, truthful, and unselfish, and someday you will be a real boy. . . ."

Pinocchio stirred and sat up. The Blue Fairy's promise had come true! Pinocchio was a real, live boy at last!

WALT DISNEY'S
DUMBO
OF THE CIRCUS

It was spring in the circus! After the long winter's rest, it was time to set out again on the open road.

"All aboard!" shouted the ringmaster. Then with a jiggety jerk and a brisk *puff-puff,* off sped Casey Jones, the locomotive. The circus was on its way!

Inside the train, Mrs. Jumbo fawned over her brand-new baby elephant.

The baby sneezed. *Ka-CHOO!* His head jerked back and his ears flapped forward. Such large ears! The other elephants snickered.

"Little Jumbo!" giggled one scornfully. "Little *Dumbo* . . . that's his name!"

Dumbo sniffed and toddled toward his mother. Tenderly Mrs. Jumbo picked him up, wrapped her trunk around him, and rocked him to sleep.

It was dark and rainy when Casey Jones pulled into the city. Runways clanked down. Horses pulled wagons, and elephants lugged tent poles. Mrs. Jumbo worked while her baby held fast to her tail.

By morning, the rain had stopped, the tent was up, and the circus was ready for the big parade through town. The crowds on the sidewalk cheered.

Then, suddenly, the crowd began to laugh. "Look at that animal with the draggy ears! He can't be an elephant . . . he must be a clown!"

Dumbo toddled along, trying to go faster, but he stumbled. He tripped over his ears. Now the crowd laughed even louder. Mrs. Jumbo scowled at them, picked Dumbo up, and carried him with her trunk the rest of the way.

After the parade, people streamed into the circus

grounds. Some noisy boys came over to Mrs. Jumbo's stall. One of them reached over the rope and pulled Dumbo's ear. Enraged, Mrs. Jumbo snatched the boy up with her trunk, laid him across the rope, and spanked him. Then she sprayed all the boys with water.

Soon Mrs. Jumbo was chained in a prison wagon.

A sign on the wagon said: DANGER! MAD ELEPHANT!

The next day, the ringmaster made Dumbo into a clown and used him in the most ridiculous act in the show. He had to jump from the top of a blazing cardboard house into a firemen's net. The audience thought it was a great joke. Dumbo felt humiliated.

That night, when Dumbo entered the elephant tent, the big animals turned their backs on him. "He's a disgrace to us all!" they agreed. Tears welled up in Dumbo's eyes.

Hidden in a pile of hay, Timothy Mouse saw the whole thing. "Don't listen to them," he said to Dumbo. "We'll make you the star of the show," said Timothy. "You'll be flying high!"

Dumbo flapped his ears hopefully.

"Say! That's not a bad idea. Those ears are as good as wings," said Timothy. "I'll teach you to fly!"

So Dumbo and Timothy crept away from the circus to practice flying. But hard as he tried, Dumbo could not leave the ground. At last, they gave up and started back to the circus.

That night, Dumbo had a dream that he was flying as easily and gracefully as a bird! And the dream seemed so real!

When the sun arose, Timothy was the first to awaken. What was this? He and Dumbo were up in a tree!

"You and that elephant just came a-flying up!" said some crows sitting nearby. Dumbo opened his eyes and struggled to his feet. Then, with Timothy clinging to his trunk, he slipped and fell into a shallow pond down below.

"Dumbo, you can fly!" Timothy panted, and he explained how Dumbo had flown in his sleep. They practiced flying all over again. But poor Dumbo fell flat on his face every time. Timothy tried to encourage him, but nothing worked.

Then one of the crows took Timothy aside. "Flying's just a matter of believing that you can do it," the crow whispered. He plucked a black feather from his tail. "Tell Dumbo this is a magic feather. If he holds it, he can fly."

Timothy tried the trick, and moments later, Dumbo was soaring like a bird!

Dumbo and Timothy returned to the circus tent and decided to keep Dumbo's flying a secret—until the afternoon show. Soon Dumbo was in his clown costume, perched atop the cardboard house and clutching the magic feather.

The fire crackled. Dumbo jumped! But as he did, the feather slipped from his trunk. His magic was gone! Dumbo began to fall like a stone.

Timothy acted quickly. "Dumbo, the feather's a fake!" he shouted. "You can fly!"

Dumbo heard his friend and spread his ears wide. Not two feet above the net, he swooped up into the air. A gasp arose from the crowd. Dumbo was flying! Mrs. Jumbo was brought to the tent to see him fly.

News of the flying elephant spread from coast to coast, and the circus was renamed "Dumbo's Flying Circus." But best of all, Dumbo forgave everyone who had been unkind to him, for his heart was as big as his magical ears.

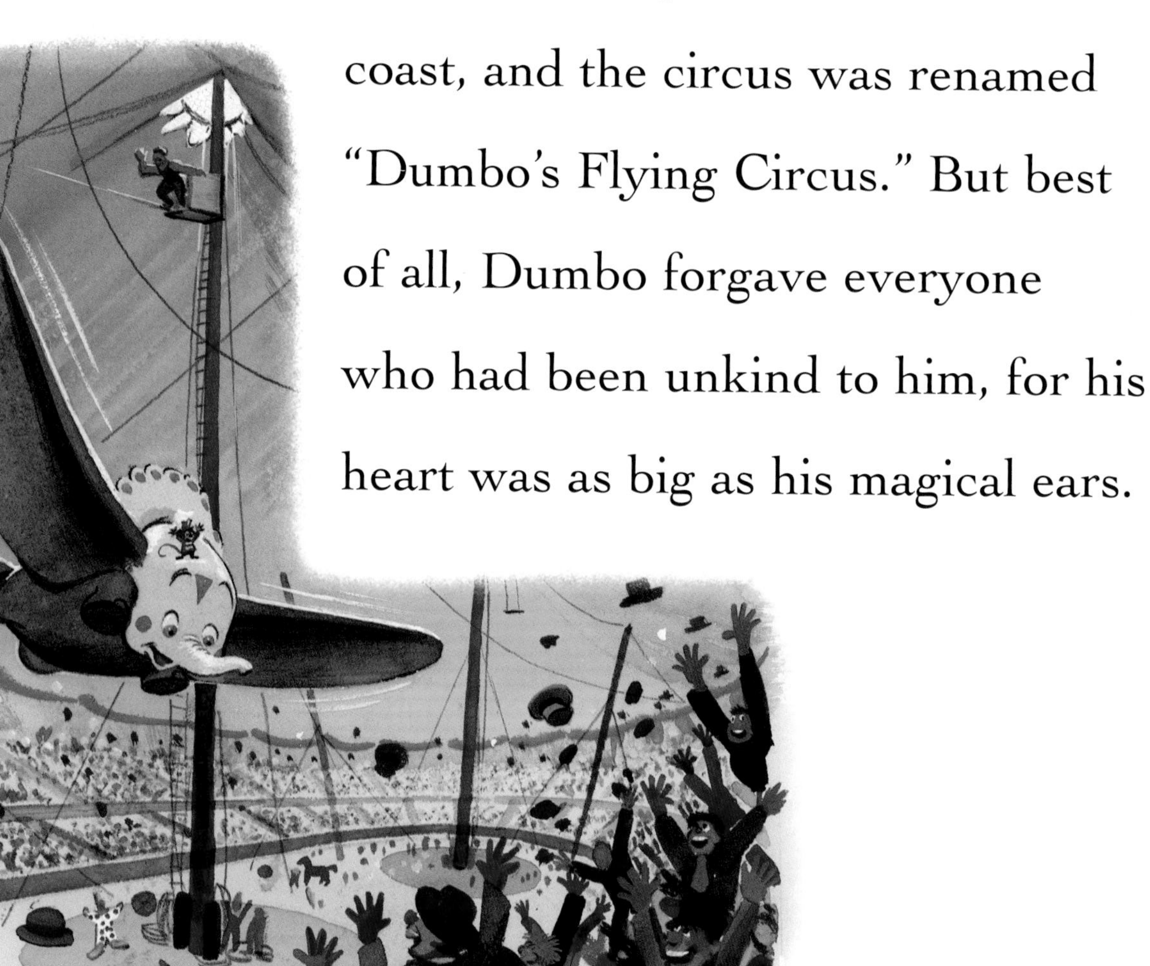

WALT DISNEY'S
101
DALMATIANS

Pongo, Perdita, and their fifteen newborn puppies lived in a cozy little house in London. Their humans, Roger and Anita, lived there, too. They all got along splendidly and were very happy.

Then one day the doorbell rang, and in came Cruella De Vil, Anita's old friend from school.

"Fifteen puppies!" Cruella cried. "How marvelous! Just name your price, dear."

"Oh, Cruella," Anita said with a gasp, "I'm afraid we can't give them up." Nanny tried to pull the puppies' basket away from Cruella.

"Don't be ridiculous," said Cruella. "You can't possibly afford to keep them."

But Roger and Anita would not budge. Furious, Cruella stormed out of the house.

One night a few weeks

later, Pongo and Perdita went out for a walk with Roger and Anita. The puppies were at home, asleep in their basket. Suddenly, two men burst into the house! They put the puppies into a big bag. Then they sped away in a truck.

The newspapers were full of the news the next morning. "DOGNAPPING! FIFTEEN PUPPIES STOLEN!"

Cruella grinned as she read the paper. Her plan had worked perfectly!

The next evening, Pongo and Perdita went on another walk with Roger and Anita. Together, they barked long and loud to spread the sad news about the dognapping. They wanted all the dogs of London to be on the lookout for their puppies.

The news traveled quickly out to the country. A bloodhound named Towser heard the shocking story. "Ruff! Ruff!" he barked, trying to reach the Colonel, an Old English sheepdog that lived nearby.

The Colonel heard the message. His friend Sergeant Tibs the cat said he had recently heard puppies barking at the old De Vil place. So they went to investigate. Sure enough, when they peeked inside the window of the mansion, they saw the fifteen stolen Dalmatian puppies—along with many, many others!

There were two men in the house, guarding the puppies. Sergeant Tibs watched as Cruella De Vil arrived at the mansion in her car. Then, before she raced off again, she ordered the men to make fur coats out of the puppies!

Tibs had to do something! So he snuck inside and helped the pups escape through a hole in the wall.

The men realized that the puppies were getting away. The chase was on! Just then, Pongo and Perdita

crashed through the window. They had found their way to the De Vil mansion with the help of many friends. They fought off the men and got away safely.

Outside, the dogs thanked the Colonel and Tibs,

and then headed for London. Pongo and Perdita led the way, with all ninety-nine of the pups following them. They walked on a frozen river for as long as they could so they wouldn't leave any paw prints behind.

But that didn't throw Cruella off their trail.

"Here are their tracks, heading straight for the village!" she cried. She ordered her men to take the side roads while she took the main road to the village.

A kind black Labrador in the village had found a

ride home for the Dalmatians, inside a moving van. As the dogs waited in a shed for the van to be ready, Cruella's car pulled up outside! How would they escape now?

Pongo had a plan. He, Perdita, and the puppies rolled around in a pile of soot. Soon they all looked like black Labradors!

Then they crept outside and got into the van. The disguises were working! Cruella didn't even look their way—until some snow fell on one of the pups and washed the soot off.

"There they go!" shouted Cruella.

As the van pulled away, Cruella chased after it in her car. So did her two henchmen in their truck. They tried to force the van off the road, but instead, the henchmen crashed into Cruella's car. The three villains

tumbled off the road and into a snowbank.

Finally, the dogs made it home to London. Roger and Anita were so happy to see them safe and sound.

As Nanny cleaned the soot off the puppies with her duster, she noticed there were many, many more of them. Roger,

Anita, and Nanny counted them all up. Including Pongo and Perdita, they now had 101 Dalmatians!

"We'll buy a big place in the country!" said Roger, excitedly.

So that's exactly what they did. Roger, Anita, Nanny, Pongo, Perdita, and all the puppies lived there happily ever after.

WALT DISNEY'S
Bootle Beetle's Adventure

Grandpa Bootle Beetle sat back and let out a sigh.

"Yes," he said, "I had some real adventures in my day. Why, I remember one time long ago. . . ."

Then he was off, and this is the wonderful story he told.

"I was just a young bug then, eager to roam.

So with my pack upon my back, I set out from my home.

"But it wasn't long before I stopped, for the ground ahead suddenly dropped.

"Hmm, I thought, surveying for a moment or two, this looks like the print of a giant shoe.

"Then, as I stood pondering, a great dark shadow came sweeping by. I jumped to one side, and just in time. When I came down, I let out a hoot, for I'd landed squarely on a giant's boot!

"Up and down I swooped and swayed. And when the dizzy ride stopped, I climbed off and tottered away.

"Then what should I see, right in front of me? A roaring fire!

"'A forest fire!' I shouted, and I turned and ran—straight into the giants' frying pan. Of course, I didn't realize it then, but they weren't giants—they were men!

"Soon I was lifted up through the air—higher and higher. Then down went the pan—right on top of the fire!

"There was no place to jump to. And I could not fly. Oh, no! thought I. I'll surely fry!

"But as I sizzled—*spatter-splat*—down came the rain and fixed all that.

"The flames beneath me hissed and died. As for me, I mopped my brow and sighed.

"But that's not the end of the story.

"The frying pan was lifted, and up I went, and soon I found myself on a shelf in a tent.

"It was a long, long way to jump (without acquiring a scratch or bump). So it looked as if I had to stay.

"Then I heard a voice!

"'Hang on to that bootle beetle there,' it said. 'Those creatures are very rare.'

"Down came a hand through the air, as if to trap me then and there.

"I closed my eyes. One, two, three—I jumped!—and landed *thumpety, bump, ker-thump!*

"When I came to, I saw daylight, and so I ran away with all my might.

"So let that be a lesson to you—if you're smaller than an inch or two, beware of giant hands and frying pans. And to bootle beetles everywhere: Be alert wherever you go, because we are very rare, you know."

Walt Disney's
The Old Mill

It was early spring when the mother and father robin found the old mill.

"This is the place for our nest," said the father robin, as they flew inside.

"Let us start right away," said the mother robin. "I like it here."

So they chose a hollow in the old mill wheel's stone base, and there they built their nest.

Soon the mother robin laid five speckled eggs.

"We have five speckled eggs in our nest," sang the father robin to the ducks swimming on the pond and the frogs hiding under the lily pads outside the old mill. Then he hunted for the plumpest, most delicious worms to take home to the mother robin.

So the spring days drifted softly past the old mill.

"We shall not have much longer to wait," said the mother robin one evening.

"Soon our eggs will hatch," said the father robin.

But that night, a storm came sweeping across the meadow. With a creak, the windmill sails began to turn in the cruel wind, while inside, the old mill wheel rumbled.

"A storm!" chirped the mother robin, as the great

mill wheel came clanking toward the nest. "What shall we do?"

"We shall have to leave the nest if the wheel comes closer," said the father robin, ruffling his feathers in alarm.

"Leave our precious eggs?" chirped the mother robin. "Oh, never!"

So the robins huddled together in the creaking darkness. Shutters banged. Beating rain forced its way inside and sent the mice scampering to find new holes.

Each time the mill wheel creaked, it seemed as if it would be the last moment for the nest. But the robins stayed, keeping their eggs warm and dry.

Finally, the storm in its fury flung a lightning bolt straight at the mill's flailing arms. With a groan, the mill slouched down on its foundation. Its broken sails creaked to a stop. The mill wheel halted. And the robins' nest was safe.

The storm swept on across the meadow, and in the calm it left behind, the old mill slept.

Soon it was morning.

"We have five hungry babies in our nest," chirped the father robin to the ducks and the frogs outside the mill, as he hunted for big, plump, delicious worms.

"And how is the world outside, now that the storm

is over?" asked the mother robin when the father robin returned.

"It is washed fresh and clean by the storm," said the father robin, as he fed the babies. "And the dear old mill looks more beautiful than ever." The mother robin sighed. "Let us never, never leave the dear old mill."

Walt Disney's
Peter Pan

Late one night, high above the city of London, Peter Pan and Tinker Bell flew across the sky. They stopped at the nursery window of the Darling family and crept silently inside. The Darling children — Wendy, Michael, and John — were all fast asleep.

Peter Pan had to find his shadow! He had left it behind the last time he had visited the Darling nursery. He often came and secretly listened to Wendy tell bedtime stories about Never Land, pirates, fairies, and himself—Peter Pan!

Finally, Peter found the shadow inside a dresser drawer. But when he tried to catch it, the shadow flew away. Peter chased it around the room, knocking over a table and waking Wendy.

Before long, Peter

Pan had convinced Wendy to come back to Never Land with him!

"Oh, Peter, it would be so wonderful!" said Wendy with a gasp. "I'm so happy I think I'll give you a kiss." She stepped up to Peter Pan and puckered her lips. But just then, something

yanked her back by the hair. It was Tinker Bell! The tiny pixie was already jealous of Wendy.

"Stop it, Tink!" scolded Peter, chasing the pixie around the room. Soon Michael and John were also awake. They wanted to come to Never Land, too.

So Peter Pan sprinkled some of Tinker Bell's pixie dust over the children and told them to think happy thoughts. "You can fly!" said Peter.

Soon they were soaring through the sky, heading for Never Land.

At last, the children looked down and saw golden rainbows, blue waterfalls, and mermaids singing in a lagoon. It was the most beautiful place they had ever seen.

"Oh, Peter," said Wendy happily. "It's just as I've always dreamed it would be."

There were beaches and deep forests and, of course, there was a pirate ship! Yes, this indeed was Never Land!

Peter Pan led the children to Hangman's Tree, the secret hideout where he lived with his good friends, the Lost Boys. Then, while John and Michael went off to explore the island with the Lost Boys, Peter Pan and Wendy went to visit the mermaids in Mermaid Lagoon.

It was there that Peter Pan spied the Indian

princess, Tiger Lily, tied up in the rowboat of the evil Captain Hook and his first mate, Mr. Smee. Captain Hook had kidnapped her! Peter and Wendy could overhear the pirate saying, "You tell me the hiding place of Peter Pan and I shall set you free." But loyal and proud Tiger Lily would not say a word.

Peter Pan and Wendy trailed Captain

Hook to Skull Rock, where Peter challenged Captain Hook to a thrilling duel. Peter was too quick for the pirate, who ended up in the water and was chased away by the Crocodile.

Peter rescued Tiger Lily and brought her safely home. The Indian Chief was so grateful, he made Peter Pan a chief, too.

As for Captain Hook, he was furious! He hatched a plan to get back at Peter Pan. First, he had his first mate capture Tinker Bell. Captain Hook tricked her into revealing the location of Peter's secret hideout. Then he locked her up inside a lantern.

As Captain Hook's band of pirates approached Hangman's Tree, the Darlings and the Lost Boys were coming outside. One by one, they were captured.

But Captain Hook still did not have Peter Pan. So he and Smee left behind a bomb, wrapped as a gift from Wendy. Soon, Peter would open it and—*ka-boom!*

"Peter Pan will save us," Wendy said to Captain

Hook, when they had all been taken back to the pirate ship.

Captain Hook roared with laughter. Then he gave the children the choice of turning into pirates or walking the plank. Wendy refused to join the pirate crew.

"As you wish," said Captain Hook. Then he pointed to the plank. "Ladies first, my dear."

Meanwhile, no one noticed that Tinker Bell had escaped from the lantern and flown off to warn Peter Pan. She felt terrible that she had caused so much trouble by revealing the location of the hideout. Now she raced back to Hangman's Tree and arrived just in time to save Peter from the gift-wrapped bomb.

Once Tinker Bell had told Peter what had happened, he raced to rescue his friends. He arrived at

Captain Hook's pirate ship just as Wendy was stepping off the end of the plank. Peter scooped Wendy up in midair and flew her to safety.

"This time you have gone too far!" Peter shouted to Captain Hook. He swooped down from the rigging, all set for a duel.

In the midst of their struggle, Captain Hook challenged Peter Pan to fight him without flying. Peter agreed. But would he be able to defeat the pirate?

Tinker Bell slashed the ropes that bound the boys. They beat the pirates, who jumped overboard. Then Peter got Hook's sword away from him, and Hook fell into the water. When the children last saw him, the evil pirate was swimming away with the Crocodile close behind.

Peter Pan took command of the pirate ship. "Hoist anchor!" he cried.

Tinker Bell sprinkled pixie dust on the deck, and the pirate ship was suddenly sailing through the skies of Never Land, heading back to London.

"Michael, John," said Wendy, "we're going home!"

Back in the nursery, Wendy waved good-bye as

Peter Pan sailed off into the night. Looking over Wendy's shoulder, her mother, Mary Darling, could not believe her eyes. Together, mother and daughter watched the ship as it sailed past the moon on its journey home . . . to Never Land.

MAKENNA